LOOK
and
LISTEN

Who's in the Garden, Meadow, Brook?

by
Dianne White

Illustrated by
Amy Schimler-Safford

MARGARET FERGUSON BOOKS

HOLIDAY HOUSE · NEW YORK

With gratitude to Lynn and Karen – friends and writers
who are always ready to look and listen to each new project.
–D.W.

For Mom and Dad and sunset walks.
–A.S.

Margaret Ferguson Books

Text copyright © 2022 by Dianne White • Illustrations copyright © 2022 by Amy Schimler-Safford
All Rights Reserved • HOLIDAY HOUSE is registered in the U.S. Patent and Trademark Office.
Printed and bound in January 2022 at C&C Offset, Shenzhen, China
The artwork was created using mixed media to include watercolor, oil paint,
embellished papers, and crayon.
www.holidayhouse.com • First Edition • 10 9 8 7 6 5 4 3 2 1
Library of Congress Cataloging-in-Publication Data
Names: White, Dianne, author. | Schimler-Safford, Amy, illustrator.
Title: Look and listen / by Dianne White ; illustrated by Amy Schimler-Safford.
Description: New York : Holiday House, 2022. | "Margaret Ferguson Books." | Audience: Ages 4 to 8. | Audience: Grades K-1
Summary: In rhyming text the reader takes a walk on a garden path, through a meadow, and along the banks of a stream,
noting the animals that are seen along the way.
Identifiers: LCCN 2021005564 | ISBN 9780823443468 (hardcover)
Subjects: LCSH: Stories in rhyme. | Nature stories. | Picture books for children. | CYAC: Stories in rhyme. | Nature—Fiction.
LCGFT: Stories in rhyme. | Picture books.
Classification: LCC PZ8.3.W58735 Lo 2022 | DDC [E]—dc23
LC record available at https://lccn.loc.gov/2021005564

ISBN: 978-0-8234-4346-8 (hardcover)

Let's go outdoors, among the trees.
Look and listen. Feel the breeze.

Stroll the path from here to there.
Sights and sounds are everywhere.

In the garden, flowers grow.
Hues of color, row on row.

Who's that buzzing? Listen. See.
A fuzzy, YELLOW busy . . .

BEE.

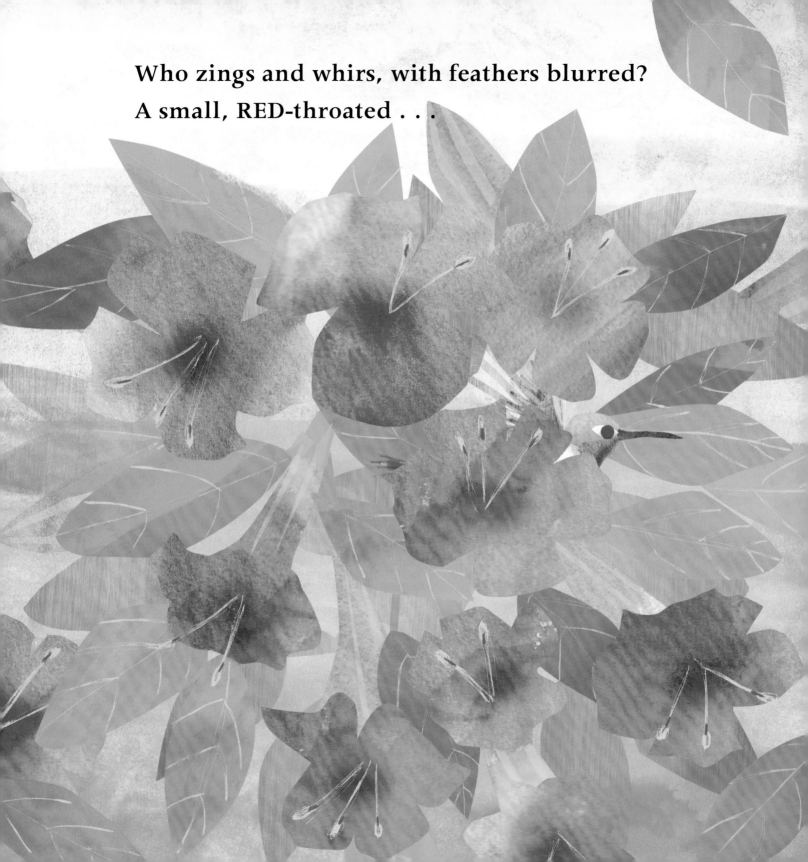

Who zings and whirs, with feathers blurred?
A small, RED-throated . . .

HUMMINGBIRD.

Whose dainty wings whisper by?
A lacy BLUE . . .

BUTTERFLY.

A sea of sighing grasses sweep
across the meadow, wide and deep.

Whose back foot stomps, loud and funny?
A GRAY and long-eared hopping . . .

BUNNY.

Whose cheerful song calls us to follow?
A bright, WHITE-bellied diving . . .

SWALLOW.

Who bounds away as we draw near?
A BROWN and spotted baby . . .

DEER.

Along the trail, a bubbling brook.
Let's wander near and have a look.

Who croaks beside a mossy log?
A GREEN and lumpy, leaping . . .

FROG.

Whose gleaming wings rustle by?
An ORANGE, glittered . . .

DRAGONFLY.

Who darts away with one quick swish?
A tiny SILVER shiny . . .

FISH.

Who knows to listen, stop, and look?

Who loves the garden, meadow, brook?

Who sings a joyful morning song?

YOU!

GARDEN

A garden is an ecosystem, or community, of living and nonliving things. Each member of the garden has a role to play—from the soil that welcomes seeds, to the plants that provide food, to the bees, birds, butterflies, and other animals that carry seeds, spread pollen, and control the population of bugs.

BUMBLEBEE

Who helps the garden grow? *Bzzz! Bzzz!* Bumblebees do. These black and yellow buzzing pollinators help spread pollen from one plant to the next. Their short, stubby wings vibrate 130 or more times per second, shaking loose the pollen from blooms, such as sunflowers.

RUBY-THROATED HUMMINGBIRD

Zip! Whiz! Whir! The ruby-throated hummingbird is an amazing acrobat—flying up, down, backwards, and forwards, even hovering in place to sip nectar. With wings that beat about 53 times per second, this tiny omnivore feeds on insects, spiders, and the nectar of flowers, such as the trumpet flower.

EASTERN TAILED-BLUE BUTTERFLY

You won't hear the eastern tailed-blue butterfly flutter by. This delicate insect, with a wingspan of about one inch, is part of the group of butterflies called gossamers. From above, the males are iridescent blue, while the females vary from blue to brown. Underneath, the wings of both are silvery gray with several eyespots. A hair-like tail on each hind wing helps deter enemies.

MEADOW

A meadow is a vital ecosystem of wide-open fields of grasses, wildflowers, and other non-woody plants. Meadows provide shelter for smaller animals—such as insects, spiders, rabbits, and birds—and larger animals—such as deer and elk.

EASTERN COTTONTAIL RABBIT

Thump, thump, thump! When distressed, the eastern cottontail rabbit hammers a warning with its hind feet. It runs to safety by zigzagging at speeds of up to 18 miles per hour. The cottontail has brown to dark gray fur and a fluffy white tail. Its keen senses of hearing, sight, and smell help the rabbit stay alert to predators.

TREE SWALLOW

Tweet-pleet-tweet! Tree swallows are social birds. They use high-pitched songs and calls to greet the morning, signal alarm, or communicate with mates. The male bird's greenish-blue iridescent back and clean, white front make it easy to spot. Female and juvenile birds are less colorful—brownish above, with the occasional hint of blue-green.

WHITE-TAILED DEER

If you hike across a meadow, don't be surprised if you pass a young white-tailed deer, called a fawn, nestled in the underbrush. Its chestnut fur, covered in white spots, serves as the perfect camouflage until it grows older. When in danger, the deer bounds away on strong, swift legs.

AMERICAN BULLFROG

Mrrrgh! Sounding almost like a mooing cow, the low call of the male American bullfrog rumbles across the shallows. This bullfrog is the largest frog in North America. With colors ranging from green to brown, often with spots on its back, the American bullfrog needs to live near water in order to survive.

BROOK

A brook is fresh, moving water, smaller than a stream. Frogs and dragonflies sometimes lay their eggs along a brook's quiet, protected banks. The baby frogs—called tadpoles—and young dragonflies—called nymphs—live underwater for a period of time before spending the remainder of their lives above the surface.

EASTERN AMBERWING

You may not *hear* this dragonfly rustle by, but you'll definitely *see* the bright orange-colored wings of the male eastern amberwing. About one inch long, with brown and yellow lines circling the abdomen, the eastern amberwing can look like a wasp. It even wiggles its abdomen and wings, imitating a wasp's movements. This adaptation, called mimicking, warns predators to stay away.

GOLDEN SHINER

Flip. Swish. Splash! Golden shiners are part of the minnow family. The smaller of these fish have transparent fins and are more silver-colored than gold. There's safety in numbers, so these minnows often swim in schools as a way to protect themselves from fish that want to eat them.